JON SCIESZKA'S TRUCKTOWN
DIZZY IZZY

WRITTEN BY JON SCIESZKA

CHARACTERS AND ENVIRONMENTS DEVELOPED BY THE

DAVID SHANNON   LOREN LONG   DAVID GORDON

ILLUSTRATION CREW:

Executive producer: TOT INDUSTRIES in association with Animagic S.L.

Creative supervisor: Nina Rappaport Brown ○ Drawings by: Dan Root ○ Color by: Christopher Oatley

Art director: Karin Paprocki

READY-TO-ROLL

ALADDIN
NEW YORK   LONDON   TORONTO   SYDNEY

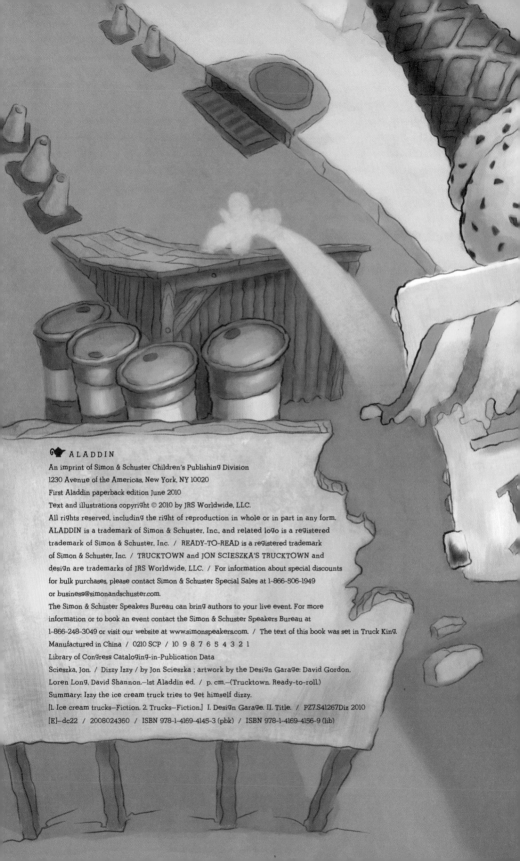

✸ ALADDIN

An imprint of Simon & Schuster Children's Publishing Division
1230 Avenue of the Americas, New York, NY 10020
First Aladdin paperback edition June 2010

The Simon & Schuster Speakers Bureau can bring authors to your live event. For more
information or to book an event contact the Simon & Schuster Speakers Bureau at
1-866-248-3049 or visit our website at www.simonspeakers.com. / The text of this book was set in Truck King.
Manufactured in China / 0210 SCP / 10 9 8 7 6 5 4 3 2 1
Library of Congress Cataloging-in-Publication Data
Scieszka, Jon. / Dizzy Izzy / by Jon Scieszka ; artwork by the Design Garage: David Gordon,
Loren Long, David Shannon.—1st Aladdin ed. / p. cm.—(Trucktown. Ready-to-roll.)
Summary: Izzy the ice cream truck tries to get himself dizzy.
[1. Ice cream trucks—Fiction. 2. Trucks—Fiction.] I. Design Garage. II. Title. / PZ7.S41267Diz 2010
[E]—dc22 / 2008024360 / ISBN 978-1-4169-4145-3 (pbk) / ISBN 978-1-4169-4156-9 (lib)

This is Izzy.

Izzy loves to get **dizzy.**

But is he?

Izzy gets
busy.

Izzy skids in a tizzy.
But Izzy is not dizzy.

Is he?

Izzy gets fizzy.
But Izzy is not dizzy.

Is he?

THEN IZZY GETS AN IDEA.

"Do you want an ice cream?
Do you want an ice cream?
Do you want an ice cream?"

Izzy whizzes.

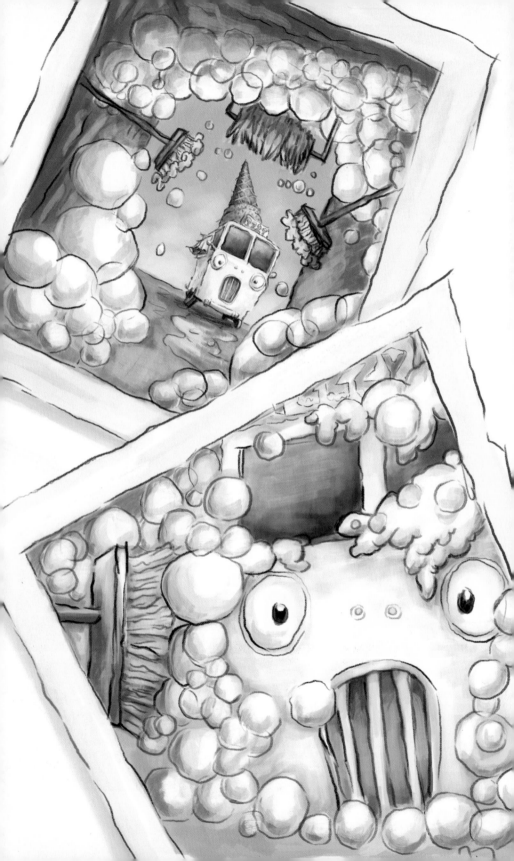

Izzy fizzes.

Izzy gets busy and fizzy
and all whizzy
in a tizzy.

Izzy is
dizzy!

But
guess
what?

Now Izzy thinks
he was fuzzy.

Was he?